501 Would You Rather and Try Not to Laugh Challenges, Christmas Edition

Contents

Part 1: Would You Rather for Kids, Christmas Edition   4

Introduction Letter to Parents   5

Introduction Letter to Children   6

Section 1: Snowflakes and Stockings: Would You Rather?   6

Section 2: Reindeer Riddles   20

Section 3: Christmas Morning Marvels: Pick Your Present   26

Section 4: Yuletide Yummies: 20 Delicious Christmas Treats   32

Section 5: Joyful Jests: 50 Incredible Xmas Jokes   58

Section 6: Oh Night Divine: 10 Awesome Christmas Songs   70

Section 7: Gift-Giving Giggles: 30 Christmas Knock-Knock Jokes   84

Section 8: Mistletoe Mysteries   96

Section 9: 50 Festive Puns for Festive Fun   100

Thank You Message   114

Part 2: Try Not to Laugh Christmas Challenge   115

Introduction Letter to Parents   116

Introduction Letter to Children   117

Section 1: Deck the Halls with Knock-Knock Classics   118

Section 2: Mistletoe Mischief - 20 Cheeky Jokes   128

Section 3: 30 Cool Christmas Quiz Questions   133

Section 4: Snowman Stand Up: 20 Classic Christmas Funnies   146

Section 5: Festive Would You Rather   152

Section 6: Tinsel Town Teasers: 20 Movie-Themed Questions   163

Section 7: Holiday Feast Funnies: 20 Fantastic Food Jokes   170

Section 8: 30 Festive Quotes for All!   175

Section 9: Wrapped in Whimsy: 20 Festive Puns   184

Section 10: 30 Christmas Tongue Twisters   190

Section 11: Silly Song Lyrics   197

Thank You Message   206

Part 1: Would You Rather for Kids, Christmas Edition

Ahoy Publications

WOULD YOU Rather for Kids

Christmas Edition

300+ Holiday-Themed Try Not To Laugh Questions and Hilarious Scenarios

Introduction Letter to Parents

Dear Guardian,

The Christmas holidays are always a great time to spend with your family, but it can also be very stressful. The pressure of having picture-perfect special moments with your family can often undermine the quality of the time you spend together. This book aims to give you something to focus on away from the glare and stress of screens and social media: A time when you can discover more about each other and just enjoy laughing together while embracing the joy of the season.

Recent studies have proven that kids with a well-developed sense of humor are likelier to be happy, optimistic, and have high self-esteem. There is also evidence that those who find the funny in most situations are more adaptable and handle change better than their more serious peers. Exploring humor together is a fun and relaxed way to connect with your child, leading to discussions about why you did or didn't find the joke funny.

Humor can expand cognitive capacity and enhance critical thinking skills, stimulating young minds and helping to promote lateral thinking. This book is packed with gentle humor, brain-busting riddles, and creative Christmas recipes to help your holidays be filled with Christmas spirit.

Introduction Letter to Children

Hi!
We hope you enjoy this book and that it brings you, your friends, and your family lots of laughter.

As well as funny would-you-rather scenarios, knock-knock jokes, and silly riddles, we've added recipes for delicious Christmas treats and songs to help you make this Christmas unforgettable.

This book is designed to be shared. Please read it with your friends and family, tell someone a festive joke, make a yummy present for your teacher or neighbor, or start a sing-along at the bus stop! We challenge you to use what's in the book to spread enough Christmas cheer to last throughout the whole year!

Dear Santa,
My Name Is _____
I am _____ years Old.
I have been very _____ this year.

My christmas Wish List is:
1. _____
2. _____
3. _____
4. _____
5. _____
With Love,

Section 1: Snowflakes and Stockings: Would You Rather?

Christmas is all about having fun with friends and family, and this is a super silly game you can play with anyone! To make it more interesting, try guessing what each other will say by writing it on paper and placing it face down on the table before they answer. Award one point for everyone who guesses correctly, and total the score at the end!

PLAYER	SCORE	TOTAL SCORE

Would you rather meet Santa or Frosty the Snowman?

Would you rather have unlimited Christmas crackers or a year's supply of candy canes?

Would you rather eat a chocolate Santa or drink hot chocolate?

Would you rather use smelly socks as a stocking or not have a stocking at all?

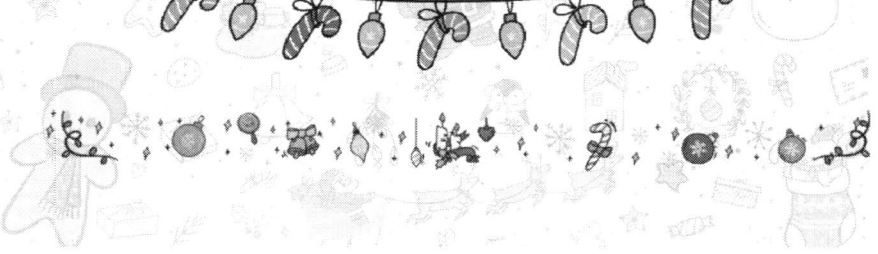

Would you rather spend a year at Santa's workshop making presents or one night delivering presents in the sleigh?

Would you rather have a hat made out of tinsel or shoes made out of wrapping paper?

Would you rather only celebrate Christmas Eve or Christmas Day?

Would you rather have three French hens or a partridge in a pear tree?

Would you rather spend Christmas in a stable in Bethlehem or a log cabin in Lapland?

Would you rather roast chestnuts over an open fire or have a snowball fight?

Would you rather eat cold turkey or drink warm cider?

Would you rather get ten small presents or one big one?

Would you rather eat Christmas dinner with no cranberry sauce or no gravy?

Would you rather have a reindeer the size of a turtle

dove or a turtle dove the size of a reindeer as a pet?

Would you rather be able to fly like Santa's reindeer or make toys like Santa's elves?

Would you rather have candy tree ornaments or a chocolate Christmas tree?

Would you rather have a white Christmas or a bright Hawaiian Christmas day?

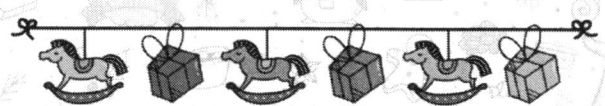

Would you rather have Santa Claus for an uncle or Buddy the Elf for a brother?

Would you rather have a bottomless box of chocolates or an endless candy cane?

Would you rather have turkey legs or candy canes for legs?

Would you rather have a bath in cranberry sauce or gravy?

Would you rather have the outside of your house covered in lights or the inside covered in decorations?

Would you rather deck the halls with boughs of holly or hang mistletoe up?

Would you rather eat a gingerbread house or live in one?

Would you rather have a ride in Santa's sleigh or go on the Polar Express?

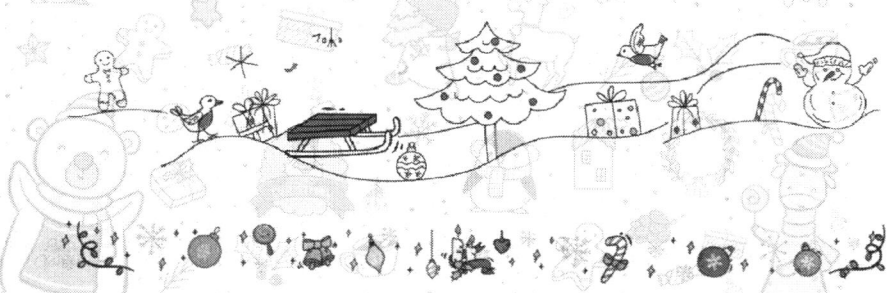

Would you rather only be able to only watch Elf or A Muppets Christmas Carol for the whole of the holidays?

Would you rather have to wear skis or ice skates throughout Advent?

Would you rather have a silent night or be rocking around the Christmas tree on Christmas Eve?

Would you rather meet Jack Frost or a magical snowman?

Would you rather have hair made of tinsel or pine needles?

Would you rather sing a Christmas song or listen to Christmas bells?

Would you rather go to school dressed as a snowman or a Christmas tree?

Would you rather have the turkey dinner or only have dessert?

Would you rather have no Christmas tree or no Christmas lights?

Would you rather go sledding or ice skating?

Would you rather have to start every sentence saying,
"It's beginning to look a lot like Christmas,"
or end every sentence saying

"Fa la la la la la la la la" for the whole month of December?

Would you rather be a giant elf or a miniature flying reindeer?

Would you rather have a nose that glows or one that looks like a cherry?

Would you rather have legs made of gingerbread or arms made of candy canes?

Would you rather have more presents in your stocking or more presents under the tree?

Would you rather open all your presents on Christmas morning or wait until after dinner?

Would you rather stay up late on Christmas Eve or get up early on Christmas morning?

Would you rather have antlers like a reindeer or a carrot for a nose?

Would you rather only have Christmas cookies or apple pie to eat all Christmas?

Would you rather only have hand-made or store-bought ornaments on your Christmas tree?

Would you rather spend Christmas day watching movies or playing board games?

Would you rather get a surprise gift or one that you chose yourself for Christmas?

Would you rather sing a Christmas carol solo or as part of a choir?

Would you rather have an elf helper or a flying reindeer?

Would you rather go on vacation at Christmas or spend it at home?

Section 2: Reindeer Riddles

Here are some more fun and games to keep you entertained until Santc comes! Take it in turns to test each other with these crazy Chris-mas riddles.

I'm not heavy, I make people stop and stare, and when it's close to Christmas, you'll see me everywhere. What am I?

Christmas lights. (They're not heavy...they're light!)

How do snowmen get to school?

On an icicle!

What comes at the end of Christmas?

The letter "S"!

Where does Jack Frost keep his money?

In a snowbank!

Where do snowmen go to dance?

A snowball!

What do you call a cat on a beach at Christmas?

Sandy Claws!

Why did the elf go on America's Got Talent?

He wanted to be a wrap star!

What do snowmen eat for breakfast?

Snowflakes!

What does December have that no other month has?

The letter "D"!

Where does Christmas come before Thanksgiving?

In the dictionary!

What do you get if you cross a tortoise with a pigeon?

A turtle dove!

Where can you find a Yule log?

Wherever Yule left it!

Why couldn't the insect sing Christmas songs?

Because he was a humbug!

What Christmas carol is about a frog and a pig?

A Muppets Christmas Carol!

Why was Santa in The Lion the Witch and the Wardrobe?

That's Narnia business!

I make everything different, yet all look the same. To all kids, I am their favorite winter game. Nothing's more exciting than seeing me at dawn; although I'm a blanket, I won't keep you warm! What am I?

Snow.

Where do Mother and Father Christmas go on vacation?

To Santa Cruz.

What do you use to strain vegetables at Christmas?

An advent colander!

I can be a man, a house, a star, or even a tree! Although they call me bread, you won't want to toast me! What am I?

Gingerbread.

When Santa leaves the North Pole to deliver presents, in

which direction does he go first?

South.

Section 3: Christmas Morning Marvels: Pick Your Present

What have you asked Santa for this Christmas? Let your imagination take flight as you decide which of these magical gifts you would like to receive. Once you've finished our list, try and make up your own fantasy gifts to choose from.

Would you rather get an invisibility cloak or a clock that lets you time travel *for Christmas?*

Would you rather have shoes that make you run *as fast as a cheetah or* shoes that make you fly *under the tree?*

Would you rather get a gift of an atlas **that allows you to travel anywhere in the world** or a TV that lets you watch **the past and future?**

Would you rather get a flying car **or** a car that turns into a submarine **for Christmas?**

Would you rather get a robot that does your chores **or** a rocket ship **as your Christmas present?**

Would you rather be gifted a pet unicorn **or** a baby dragon?

Would you rather get a pen that would be able to write the answer **to every test or** a pencil that could draw whatever **you imagined?**

Would you rather have a telescope that could let you see any planet **in the universe close up or** a phone that could ring anyone who has ever lived **as your Christmas present?**

Would you rather unwrap a game console **that could play any game or** a book that could create stories **just for you on Christmas Day?**

Would you rather get a wardrobe that allows you to travel **to a magical land or** a ring that will enable you to travel **to the spirit realm for Christmas?**

Would you rather get a candy cane that makes you fly **or** a lollypop that allows you to breathe underwater **in your stocking?**

Would you rather be gifted a pair of socks that let you climb up **anything or** gloves that allow you **to make anything?**

Would you rather get a cup that would always **be filled with whatever drink you wanted or** a lunch box that would be **filled with whatever food you fancied for Christmas?**

Would you rather get a wardrobe that would give you **your perfect outfit or** a hairdryer that would magically style **your hair as a present?**

Would you rather be given a mirror **that would answer any question or** a lamp **with a genie in it?**

Would you rather have a levitating skateboard **or** rocket boots **for Christmas?**

Would you rather have magic pants **that always have what you need in their pockets or** a magical coat that would change **to suit the weather?**

Section 4: Yuletide Yummies: 20 Delicious Christmas Treats

Chris-mas is a time for good company and good food! Here are some fantastic recipes for you to try, and they make great gifts for grandparents, teachers, and...well...anyone really!

Peppermint presents

These deliciously simple sweets are great gifts and don't require cooking.

Ingredients:

Powdered sugar
Egg white
Peppermint essence
Dark, milk, or white chocolate (optional)
Sprinkles (optional)
Food coloring (optional)

Method:

1. Sieve a cup of powdered sugar into a bowl.

2. Add a little egg white and a few drops of peppermint essence. Taste the mixture to make sure you've added enough peppermint.

3. Mix well until the mixture binds together to form a soft dough. Add the egg white a little bit at a time until you get the texture you need Top Tip: If the mixture becomes too liquid, add more icing sugar to balance it out.

4. OPTIONAL: If you want to add some color to your sweets, you can add some food coloring to the mixture at this point. You can even divide the mixture up and use different colors.

5. Divide the mixture into small balls, however big you want your sweets to be. Once you've rolled the balls, squish the tops and sides to make squares.

6. Put some parchment paper onto a baking sheet and place your little squares on the paper.

7. If you are using chocolate, ask a grown-up to help you melt the chocolate in the microwave or a bain marie.

8. Leave the chocolate to cool for a minute or two, then carefully dip the peppermint squares in the chocolate.

9. Decorate your peppermint presents with sprinkles or edible glitter, and enjoy!

Coconut Christmas Trees

Coconut cookies you don't have to bake? Yes, please!

Ingredients:

2 cups of powdered sugar
3 cups of shredded coconut
½ cup of butter, margarine, or coconut oil
2 tbsp of milk
Green food coloring
Melted white chocolate
Colorful mini sweets and/or sprinkles

Method:

1. Ask an adult to help you melt the butter /margarine/coconut oil on the stove or in the microwave.

2. Add the powdered sugar, milk, and green food coloring to a bowl.

3. Once the butter has melted, ask an adult to help pour it into the bowl.

4. Mix all your ingredients together.

5. Once it is all mixed, scoop out a bit of the mixture and roll it into a ball. Now, pinch and shape one end to make it into a cone. You might need a few attempts to get them however you want, but you can play around and reshape them as much as you want.

6. Once your "trees" are shaped, put them on a baking sheet and pop them in the fridge for 2-3 hours.

7. When they have set, melt your white chocolate and dip the tops of your tree cookies in the chocolate to make it look like snow. Turn upright and allow the chocolate to drip down the tree. Before the chocolate sets, add candies like mini M&Ms or sprinkles to make your trees look super fancy!

Gingerbread Reindeer

We all know the best thing about gingerbread men is decorating them, so why not mix it up a bit?

Ingredients:

Premade, plain Gingerbread men
Powdered sugar
Candy eyes
Chocolate chips and/or ed and black round candies

Method:

1. Turn your gingerbread man upside down.

2. Decorate the legs as antlers, the arms as ears, and the body and head as the reindeer's face!

3. Stick on the candy eyes with icing sugar, and add a chocolate chip or a round candy for the nose. Use red candies for Rudolf and black candies or chocolate chips for the rest of the gang!

4. Use a piping bag, an edible food decorating pen, or a tube of writing icing to add the detail. Top Tip: if you don't have any of

these, put your icing in a zip-lock bag and snip a tiny bit off one corner – you can now use it like a piping bag!

Edible Orange Christmas Bubbles

These look great glinting in the Christmas lights and make a super healthy, sweet snack, too!

Ingredients:

Oranges

Method:

1. Get a grown-up to help you slice the oranges. You'll want to end up with round slices that show a cross-section of the orange.

2. Either put the slices in a dehydrator or put them on a baking sheet covered in parchment paper and get a grown-up to help you put them in the oven on low heat for a couple of hours, flipping them every 30 minutes. Top Tip: Most air-fryers have a dehydrate function.

3. Once the orange slices are dry, ask an adult to put them on a cooling rack.

4. When they are dry and cool, carefully make a hole just below the peal and add a ribbon so you can hang them on the tree! The slices can be eaten as they are, sprinkled with sugar, or dipped in chocolate. Top Tip: you can use any citrus fruit, so try some blood

oranges, limes, or even grapefruit to get a good selection of colors and sizes!

Gingerbread Cookies

This classic Christmas treat is great to make with a group, especially if you have kids of different ages helping.

Ingredients:

12 oz plain flour
1 tsp baking soda
2 tsp ground ginger
1 tsp ground cinnamon
4 ½ oz butter
6 oz soft brown sugar
1 medium size egg
4 tbsp golden syrup
Powdered sugar (optional)

Method:

1. Ge~ the older kids to sift the flour, baking soda, and spices into a bowl. Then add the butter and get them to blend the mixture with their fingers until it looks like breadcrumbs.

2. Meanwhile, get the younger kids to mix the egg and golden syrup.

3. Orce both mixtures are ready, pour the egg and golden syrup into the bowl with the flour and butter and mix it – this does get messy, so you might want to use a spoon, but it's fine to do it with your hands!

4. Orce the mixture resembles dough, tip it onto a floured surface and kneed it until smooth.

5. Once the dough is ready, wrap it in clingfilm and put it in the refrigerator for around 15 minutes.

6. Once the dough is ready, ask an adult to preheat the oven to 356F or 320F for a fan oven.

7. Line two cookie trays with parchment paper.

8. This is the fun part; start molding the dough into whatever shape you want! You can roll it out and use cookie cutters to make shapes, or let your imagination go wild and create anything you like! Top Tip: make a hole in the top of your shapes so you can use them as tree decorations.

9. Once your cookie creations are ready, place them on the parchment paper and ask a grown-up to put them in the oven for you for 12-15 minutes. Once done, ask an adult to take the trays out and CAREFULLY place the cookies on a cooling rack for about 10 minutes. Warning: cookies will be hot when you take them out of the oven, so ensure you let them cool properly before eating before handling them.

10. Once your cookies are cool, you can tuck in or mix up powdered sugar to add decorations. You can then add gumdrops or sprinkles as a finishing touch!

Kids Christmas Cinnamon Rolls

If Pumpkin Spice is the flavor of fall, cinnamon has to be the taste of Christmas. These amazing no-bake cinnamon rolls are so easy to make that even the youngest members of your family can get involved.

Ingredients:

2 slices of white bread with the crusts cut off
2 tbsps. butter
2 tbsps. cinnamon sugar
2 tbsps. powdered sugar
A few drops of water

Method:

1. Flatten the bread with a rolling pin, or squish it flat with your hands (whichever way is more fun!)

2. Butter the bread and sprinkle it with cinnamon sugar.

3. Roll up the bread.

4. Get an adult to help you slice up the rolled bread.

5. Mix the confectioner's sugar with a few drops of water to make a thin icing that you can drizzle over the top. Keep adding water, a few drops at a time, until you get the consistency that you want.

6. EAT!

Marshmallow Snowmen

These festive Christmas treats are super easy to make and a lot of fun to decorate!

Ingredients:

Marshmallows
Wooden skewers

Items for decoration. You can really use your imagination for this, but we recommend fruit roll-ups, peanut butter cups, M&Ms, soft gummy candy (preferably orange), white candy coasting or melted white chocolate, pretzel sticks, and an edible brown decorating pen or a tube of writing icing.

Method:

1. Put two or three marshmallows on a skewer (make sure the Tip of the skewer is hidden in the top marshmallow. It doesn't matter what size the marshmallows are, but you could mix it up by trying some giant marshmallows or some mini marshmallows on toothpicks!

2. Optional: coast the marshmallows in white candy coating or melted white chocolate.

3. Decorate! You can do this any way you want, but we suggest using pretzel sticks for arms, fruit roll-ups for scarves, peanut butter cups for a hat, an orange gummy candy for the nose, M&Ms for buttons and draw on the eyes and mouth with an edible decorating pen or a tube of writing icing. Stick the sweets to your snowman using the candy coasting or melted chocolate.

No-Bake Fruit Cake

This delicious fruit cake would make a great gift. Alternatively, you could just eat it all yourself!

Ingredients:

Graham crackers
Raisins
Pecans or other nuts
Maraschino cherries
Marshmallows
Condensed milk

Method:

1. Soak the raisins in warm water for 30 minutes.
2. Crush up the Graham crackers.

3. Chop up the nuts and cherries.

4. Ask a grown-up to help you melt the marshmallows in the condensed milk.

5. Mix all the ingredients together.

6. Pack the mixture into a loaf pan or bowl.

7. Refrigerate overnight.

8. Top Tip: Always ask an adult to cut the cake for you. A hot knife works best for this cake, so take extra care when cutting.

Reindeer Oreo Pops

These look super cute and are fun and easy to make. Plus, you get to snack as you go...perfect!

Ingredients:

Double stuffed Oreos
Powdered sugar
Candy eyes
Mini pretzel twists
Round red candies of your choice
Sucker sticks

Method:

1. Pour some icing sugar into a bowl and mix in a tiny bit of warm water to form a thick paste.

2. Separate a double-stuffed Oreo.

3. Dip the end of a sucker stick in the powdered sugar paste and push it into the cream side of the Oreo.

4. Push the Oreo back together and allow it to set (you can put it in the refrigerator or freezer to speed it up.)

5. Make up as many Oreos on sticks as you want, and while they're setting, break the mini pretzels up to make antler shapes. Keep all the shapes you want, and eat any that don't look right!

6. Once the Oreos have set, you can add the antlers. Dip the end of one of the pretzel antlers in the icing sugar paste and stick it to the top of the Oreo. Then, add the candy eyes and red candy nose using the powdered sugar paste as glue. Allow them all to set, and you're done!

Pretzel Snowflakes

These sweet and salty snacks look amazing, and you can turn them into pretzel pops or edible Christmas decorations!

Ingredients:

Melted white chocolate or white candy melts
Mini pretzels
White and silver sprinkles and/or edible glitter

Method:

1. Line a cookie sheet or baking tray with parchment paper.

2. Ask an adult to help you melt the white chocolate or candy melts in the microwave or a bain marie.

3. Once melted, add the mini pretzels and stir to make sure all the pretzels are evenly coated.

4. Lift the pretzels out with a fork and shake off any excess chocolate.

5. Put them on the tray and pop them in the freezer for 5 minutes to set.

6. Once they've set, dip them in chocolate again and lay four at a time onto the tray. Push them together in a symmetrical shape. You don't have to use the same shape every time; just make sure all four pretzels are touching each other. Top Tip: Use pretzel sticks to make even more elaborate snowflakes!

7. Once you're happy with the shape, blob some more chocolate in the center or at any point that you think needs strengthening.

8. Add sprinkles and glitter to decorate your snowflakes

9. Leave them on the counter to set, or pop them in the freezer if you don't want to wait too long!

10. Top Tip: use more chocolate to add a sucker stick and turn them into pretzel pops, or wait until they are completely set and tie a ribbon onto them to make edible decorations.

No-Bake Christmas Brownies

These easy-to-make brownies are super festive and fancy, but the best thing is they're also kind of healthy!

Ingredients:

½ cup of nut butter

I packed cup of chopped dates

1/3 cup cocoa powder

½ tsp vanilla extract

¼ teaspoon of salt

½ cup of chocolate chips

Powdered sugar

Some sprigs of fresh rosemary

Method:

1. Mix the nut butter, dates, cocoa powder, vanilla extract, and salt in a food processor.

2. Blend until smooth.

3. Stir the chocolate chips into the mixture.

4. Line a baking tin with parchment paper and press the mixture into the tin.

5. Put the tin in the freezer for 30-40 minutes.

6. With the help of an adult, cut the brownies into squares once the mixture is set.

7. Stick a small sprig of rosemary into each one (to look like a little Christmas tree!), then sprinkle powdered sugar over the top.

Melted Snowmen

These are a fun alternative to Christmas cookies and would look great alongside the marshmallow snowmen!

Ingredients:

White melting chocolate
Candy eyes
Peanut butter cups
Orange Jimmies
Red Hot candy
Pretzel sticks

Method:

1. Ask an adult to help you melt the chocolate.

2. Drip the melted chocolate into "pools" onto a baking sheet covered in parchment paper.

3. Add the snowman's face! We suggest using a peanut butter cup for a hat, candy eyes, orange Jimmies for the nose, Red Hot's for

buttons, and pretzel sticks for arms, but you can use whatever candies you think would work.

4. Leave to set either on the counter or in the refrigerator.

Cheeky Elf's Popping Snowballs

Those cheeky elves love throwing snowballs, but you won't want to throw these anywhere but into your mouth!

Ingredients:

½ cup of butter
1 ½ cups of desiccated coconut
½ cup of powdered sugar
¾ cup of condensed milk
White or blue popping candy

Method:

1.   Ask an adult to help you melt the butter.

2.   Add the coconut, condensed milk, and powdered sugar to a bowl and mix.

3.   Add the butter to the bowl and give it a good mix. If the mixture looks a bit too wet, add more coconut or icing sugar until it holds together.

4.　　Roll the mixture into balls, then roll the balls in the popping candy and leave them in the fridge to set.

Strawberry Santa Hats

These are a delicious and quick snack for any age.

Ingredients:

Cookies
Strawberries
Whipped cream

Method:

1. Ask a grown-up to slice off the tops of the strawberries.

2. Lay out how many cookies you want to use – it doesn't matter which type of cookie you use, so just go with your favorite!

3. Put a blob of cream in the middle of each biscuit using a piping bag of whipped cream or spray cream.

4. Stick the strawberry, flat-side down, onto the blob of cream.

5. Add some cream around the base of each strawberry and a small blob on top to make the hat bobble.

6. The only thing left is to eat them!

Candy Sleighs

These make great gifts for friends and family.

Ingredients:

Candy canes
Assorted candy bars
Ribbon
Glue dots

Method:

1. Lay two candy canes next to each other, with the "hook" facing up.

2. Put the biggest candy bar onto the candy canes and use the glue dots to keep them in place. Make sure you have brought candy canes that are individually wrapped in cellophane so the glue doesn't go directly on the candy!

3. Stack other candy bars on top of the first one.

4. Wrap a ribbon around the whole lot!

5. Top Tip: You can wrap your candy bars in Christmas paper and add a bow to the top to make your sleigh super fancy!

Gumdrop Snowflakes

Cute, sweet, and fun to make – you can't go wrong with this Christmas candy craft!

Ingredients:

Gumdrops – large and small
Toothpicks

Method:

1. Carefully thread three small gumdrops onto a toothpick. You can use whatever colors you like, but we suggest using red, green, and white to add to the Christmassy feel.

2. Repeat 5 times.

3. Get a large gumdrop, and stick the 5 prepared toothpicks around the edge of the large gumdrop.

4. Add a ribbon if you want to use them as decorations, or wrap them in cellophane as a gift.

Nutter Butter Holiday Characters

Create these simple and creative holiday characters to add a Christmas twist to this classic peanut butter cookie.

Ingredients:

Nutter Butters
Melted white chocolate
Chocolate chips
Red round candy.
Candy eyes
Mini pretzel twists
Red sparkling sugar
Mini marshmallows

Method:

1. You can make three characters with this recipe: snowmen, Santa, and a reindeer.

2. To make the snowman, get an adult to help you melt the chocolate. Dip the Nutter Butter in the white chocolate and put it on a baking sheet covered in parchment paper. Add chocolate chips for the eyes and buttons. Leave to set. Top Tip: Use a Twizzler for a scarf!

3. To make Santa, dip the top of the Nutter Butter into the melted white chocolate, then dip it in the red sparking sugar. Add a mini marshmallow as a bobble, and you have Santa's hat! Dip the other end of the Nutter Butter in the melted chocolate for his beard. Stick on the candy eyes and a red candy nose using the melted chocolate. Leave to set.

4. To make the reindeer, open up the Nutter Butter and stick the mini pretzel twists to make the antlers. Use the melted chocolate to hold them in place, and stick the two halves of the cookie back together. Stick some candy eyes on using the white chocolate, then use either a red candy or a chocolate chip for the nose.

Ice Cream Cone Christmas Trees

Easy and effective, these cones aren't just for ice cream!

Ingredients:

Sugar cones
Green icing
Sprinkles and other candies for decorating

Method:

1. Spread the green icing onto the ice cream cone. Top Tip: Spread the icing from the Tip down, or use a piping bag to make a spiky tree.

2. Decorate with whatever sprinkles or candy that you think look like good tree decorations. You could use star sprinkles, pearl candies, M&Ms, or anything else you want.

Edible Pine Cones

These pine cones look so realistic that you might have a hard time convincing people that they're edible! Oh well, all the more for you to eat!

Ingredients:

Chex Chocolate cereal
Pretzel sticks
Peanut butter
Chocolate and hazelnut spread
Softened butter
Powdered sugar

Method:

1. Mix $\frac{1}{2}$ cup of peanut butter with $\frac{1}{4}$ cup of chocolate and hazelnut spread, 3 tbsp of soft butter, and 1 cup of powdered sugar.

2. Mold some of the paste mixture around a pretzel stick, making a rough cone shape and leaving the tip free.

3. Stand the pretzel stick upright on a plate with the bare tip at the top.

4. Holding the tip, start placing the cereal into the paste mixture, starting at the bottom, by pressing one corner of the square cereal piece into the paste. Make a symmetrical pattern, staggering the pieces as you go up.

5. As you get to the top, ask an adult to help you cut the cereal into small triangles to make the topmost pinecone scales.

6. Optional: When you're done, you can ask an adult to cut the top of the pretzel stick using kitchen scissors. Then, add another dollop of the peanut butter mixture and add a few more small triangle pieces to finish it off. Alternatively, you can leave a bit of pretzel showing, depending on how you think it looks.

7. Dust the finished pinecone with powdered sugar for a snowy effect.

8. To eat, pull it apart piece by piece!

Chimney Cup Cakes

Decorate cupcakes to look like Santa and his elves are diving down a chimney.

Ingredients:

Plain cupcakes
1 cup of unsalted butter
1 ½ cups of icing sugar
2 tsp vanilla extract
Black, green, and white fondant icing
Peppermint sticks
Strawberry pencils
Gold pearl sprinkles
Plain paper

Method:

1. Beat the butter, vanilla, and icing sugar together until blended. If the mixture is a bit stiff, you can add one or two tbsp of warm water.

2. Add the frosting to the cupcakes. Make sure you put it on thick enough that you will be able to push the "legs" into it.

3. Ask an adult to help you cut the strawberry pencils and peppermint sticks into 4cm lengths.

4. To make Santa's legs: Mold the black fondant icing into boot shapes around the ends of the strawberry pencils and white fondant around the tops of the boots.

5. To make elf legs: Mold the green fondant into elf boot shapes around the ends of the candy canes. Add a gold pearl sprinkle to the Tip of each boot using some icing.

6. Leave the legs to set.

7. Meanwhile, trace over our chimney template below. Color the chimney in and ask a grown-up to help you cut it out and glue it together to make a sleeve.

8. Put a chimney sleeve around each cupcake.

9. Add the "legs" just before serving.

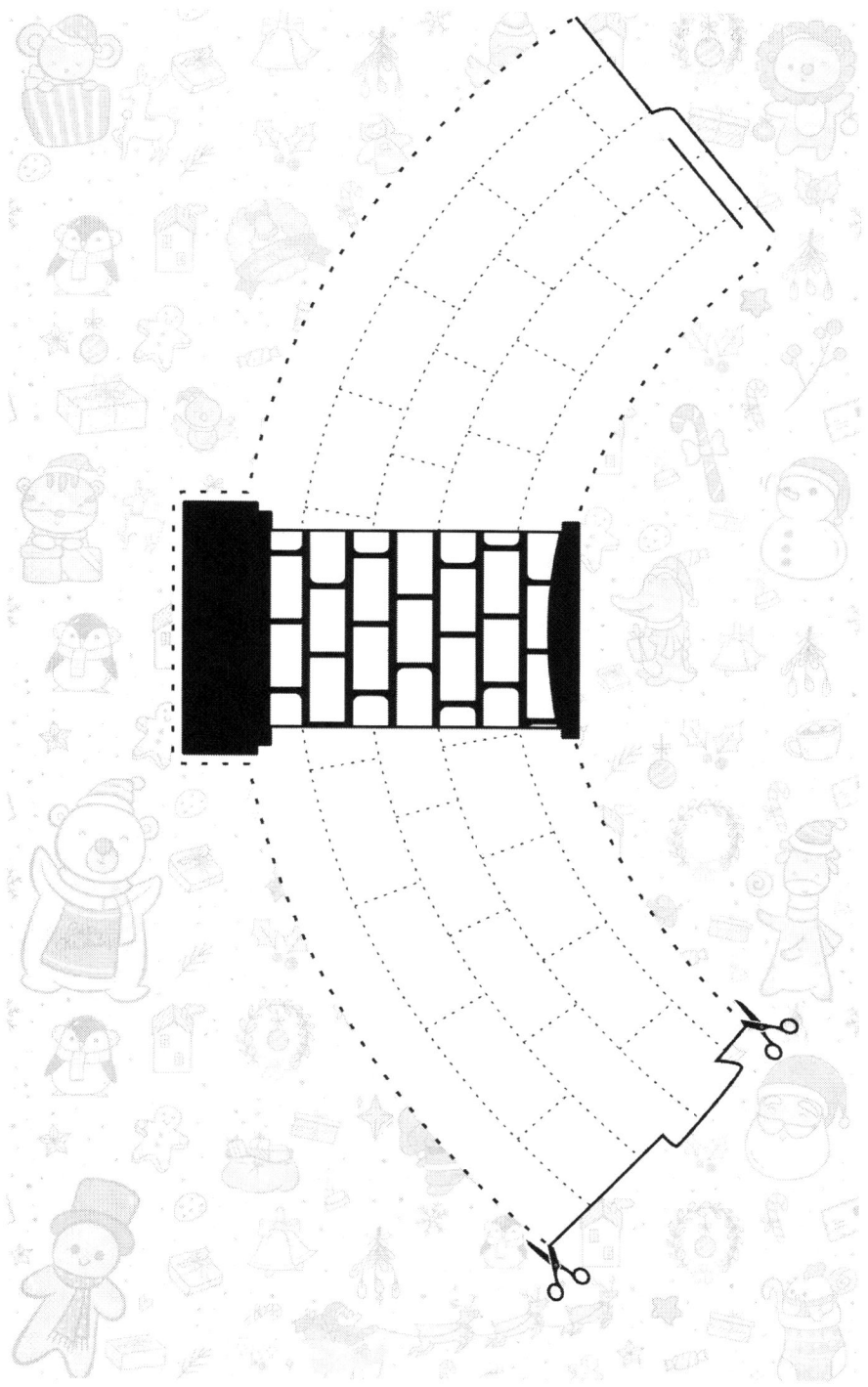

Section 5: Joyful Jests: 50 Incredible Xmas Jokes

They say that laughter is the greatest gift, so treat your friends and family this Christmas and tell them a joke or two!

What do you get when you cross a Christmas tree with an iPad?

A pineapple!

What is the first thing that elves use in school?

The elf-abet!

Why did the Christmas cookie go to the doctor?

It felt crummy!

Why did the Christmas tree go to the barber?

It needed a trim!

Why did Santa keep praising his elves?

To raise their elf-esteem!

How do Spanish sheep say Merry Christmas?

Fleece Navidad!

Why did the toys call their union of Christmas Eve?

They all got sacked!

Why did Santa go to the doctor?

He had tinsel-itis!

Where does Santa keep his suits?

In the Claus-et!

Why is it cold at Christmas?

Because it's in Decembrrrrrrr!

Why are snowmen always invited to parties?

They're cool!

What did the reindeer do when he lost his tail?

He got some re-tail therapy!

How do elves take pictures?

They take elf-ies!

What does Santa call his coffee breaks?

A Santa pause!

Which reindeer works on Valentine's Day as well as Christmas Eve?

Cupid!

What is the Christmas fairy's favorite subject in school?

Chemis-tree!

What do you call a duck at Christmas?

A Christmas quacker!

What did one snow globe say to the other?

I feel a little shaken!

What did the director say after he finished filming a documentary about Christmas presents?

That's a wrap!

What is Elf on the Shelf's favorite Christmas movie?

Home a gnome!

Buddy the Elf was the best in his class; in fact,

he was head and shoulders above the rest!

Why do people think the Grinch is such a good actor?

Because he always steals the show!

Why did the snowman go to Hollywood?

Because he wanted to get into the snow business!

Why should you always watch a bad movie on Christmas day?

Because everyone loves a Turkey at Christmas!

Why are worn Christmas socks like all Hallmark Christmas movies?

You can't tell them apart, and they stink!

I still have the carol singers from last Christmas at my house. I have no idea what figgy pudding is,

but they won't go until they've got some!

What Is a Christmas tree's favorite candy?

Orna-mints!

What did the stamp say to the Christmas card?

Stick with me, and we'll go far!

Why are Christmas plants the most intelligent?

Because they get an Ivy League education.

What did Mrs. Claus say when the gingerbread man hurt his knee?

Have you tried icing it?

What rock band does the Grinch hate the most?

The Who!

Why did no one want to buy Donner and Blitzen?

They were two deer!

What do you call an elf that just won the lottery?

wELFy!

What do you call a Snowman in July?

A puddle!

What is a Christmas tree's favorite lotion?

Tannen-Balm!

Why are Christmas presents so clever?

Because they're gifted!

What does Jack Frost cook on the barbeque?

Ice-berg-ers!

What did one cow say to the other at Christmas?

Moooey Christmas!

What did the Christmas tree say to the ornament?

Why are you always just hanging around?

Where does Santa stay when he's on holiday?

At a ho-ho-hotel!

What sandwiches does Mrs. Claus pack for Santa on Christmas Eve?

Peanut butter and jolly!

What did the snowman say to his friend, who was getting angry?

Chill out!

What happened to Rudolf when he didn't turn in his paper on the origins of Christmas?

He went down in history!

What is Jack Frost's favorite cereal?

Ice Krispies!

Why should you always check the money of an elf who pays you in cash?

They're always short!

Where does Santa keep his suits?

In the Claus-et!

What should you give your parents for Christmas?

A list of what you want!

What goes red, white, red, white, red, white?

Santa rolling down a hill!

Why are Christmas trees so bad at knitting?

They always drop their needles!

Why did the red-nosed reindeer hold the door open for Mrs. Claus?

It would have been Rudolf him not to!

Section 6: Oh Night Divine: 10 Awesome Christmas Songs

We all love trolling the ancient Yuletide carol at Christmas, so here's a selection of songs so you can strike the harp, join the chorus, and sing we joyous together, heedless of the wind and weather!

Rudolph the Red-Nosed Reindeer

By Johnny Marks

Rudolph the red-nosed reindeer,
Had a very shiny nose,
And if you ever saw it,
You would even say, "It glows!"

All of the other reindeer,
Used to laugh and call him names,
They never let poor **Rudolph,**
Join in any reindeer game.

Then, one foggy Christmas Eve,
Santa came to say:
**"Rudolph, with your nose so
bright,
Won't you guide my sleigh
tonight?"**

Then, all the reindeer loved
him,
And they shouted out with
glee,
**Rudolph the red-nosed
reindeer,**
You'll go down in history!

Ring Those Christmas Bells

By Peggy Lee

Some folks like to sing a
Christmas song,
But I like Christmas bells that
go ding-dong!
**Jingle-jangle, ding-a-ling, or
just bing-bong,**
I love to hear them ring!

Chorus:
**So ring those Christmas bells
(ding-dong-ding)#**
Ring those Christmas bells
(bing-bong-bing)
While they chime, we'll have a
happy time,
So ring those Christmas bells!
Ding-dong-ding-dong

**Up above, the stars are clear
and bright,**
While all around, the snow is
soft and white

Santa and his reindeer soon will be in sight
And you will hear him sing...

Chorus
Oh, the music of an open sleigh,
When every jolly jingle seems to say
Happy, happy, happy, happy holiday,
Oh, come on and join the fun!
Chorus

Jolly Santa Claus

Join in with the actions written in bold!

Santa Claus is big and fat; pat your belly.
He wears black boots and a big red hat; pretend to pull on boots and put on a hat.
His nose is read, just like a rose; point to your nose.
And he is jolly from his head to his toes; pat your head and touch your toes!

When Santa Got Stuck Up the Chimney!

By Jimmy Grafton

When Santa got stuck up the
chimney,
He began to shout:
**"You girls and boys won't get
any toys,
If you don't pull me out!"**

"There's soot on my back,
And my beard's all black,
My nose is tickling, too!"
**When Santa got stuck up the
chimney,
Achoo, Achoo, Achoo!**

Santa Shark

By Brett Jubinville

Santa Shark, ho ho ho ho ho ho!
Santa Shark, ho ho ho ho ho ho!
Santa Shark, ho ho ho ho ho ho!
Santa Shark!

Reindeer Sharks, do do do do do do!
Reindeer Sharks, do do do do do do!
Reindeer Sharks, do do do do do do!
Reindeer Sharks!

Elf Sharks, do do do do do do!
Elf Sharks, do do do do do do!
Elf Sharks, do do do do do do!
Elf sharks!
Load the sleigh, do do do do do do!

Load the sleigh, do do do do do do!
Load the sleigh, do do do do do do!
Load the sleigh!
Its Christmas!

Christmas Time

Join in with the actions in bold!

See the snowflakes falling;

Wiggle your fingers like falling snowflakes.

See the candles glow; Hold up one finger like a candle.

See the wreaths upon the door; Draw a circle shape with your finger.

It's Christmas time, I know!

We Wish You a Merry Christmas (with actions!)

Join in the actions in bold!

We wish you a Merry Christmas,
We wish you a Merry Christmas,
We wish you a Merry Christmas,
And a Happy New Year!

Now, let's all do a little jumping; Jump.
Now, let's all do a little hopping; Hop.
Now, let's all do a little dancing; Dance.
And now we all stop!

Keep adding verses yourself, and take turns to sing the action that everyone has to do! For example, "Now let's all touch our toes" or "Now let's all do a little stamping."

I'm a Little Santa

Sung to the tune of "I'm a little teapot."

I'm a little Santa, short and fat,

Here's my beard, and here's my sack,

When it's Christmas Eve, I ride my sleigh,

With a Ho Ho Ho! I'm on my way!

Frosty the Snowman

By Walter Rollins and Steve Nelson

Frosty the snowman,
Was a jolly happy soul,
With a corncob pipe and a
button nose,
**And two eyes made out of
coal.**

Frosty the snowman,
Was a fairy tale, they say,
He was made of snow, but the
kids all know,
How he came to life one day.

There must have been some
magic in it,
That old silk hat they found,
For when they placed it on his
head,
He began to dance around!

Oh, Frosty the Snowman,
Was alive as he could be,
And the children say he could
laugh and play,
Just the same as you and me!

Let it Snow on Christmas Day

By Roger W. Wade

Make it snow, make it snow,
make it snow this Christmas,
Never let it stop.
Make it snow, make it snow,
make it snow this Christmas,
Round my chimney top.
**Lots of ice on the lake just to
make this Christmas,
One for us to play:**

Make it snow, make it snow,
make it snow, make it snow,
**Make it snow on Christmas
Day!"**

Section 7: Gift-Giving Giggles: 30 Christmas Knock-Knock Jokes

Feast on our selection of knock-knock jokes that would even put a smile on the Grinch's face!

Knock-knock.
Who's there?
Dan.
Dan who?
Dan-cer, Dasher, Prancer, Vixen, Comet, Cupid, Donner, and Blitzen **have you seen Rudolf?**

Knock-knock.
Who's there?
Wilma.
Wilma who?
Wilma presents be good this year?

Knock-knock.
Who's there?
Oh, Holly!
Oh, Holly who?
Oh, Holly night, the stars are brightly shining!

Knock-knock.
Who's there?
Mat.
Mat who?
Mat-ching Christmas sweaters for me and you!

Knock-knock.
Who's there?
Olive.
Olive who?
Olive the other reindeer, used to
laugh and call him names...

Knock-knock.
Who's there?
Abby.
Abby who?
Abby Holidays!

Knock-knock.
Who's there?
Gladys.
Gladys who?
Gladys me who's not making
Christmas dinner!

Knock-knock.
Who's there?
Izzy.
Izzy who?
Izzy been yet? Has Santa left us presents?

Knock-knock.
Who's there?
Wanda.
Wanda who?
Wanda what I'm getting for Christmas this year!

Knock-knock.
Who's there?
Santa.
Santa who?
Santa Christmas card, did you get it?

Knock-knock.
Who's there?
Dec.
Dec who?
Deck the halls with boughs of holly!

Knock-knock.
Who's there?
Wayne.
Wayne who?
Wayne a manger!

Knock-knock.
Who's there?
Luke.
Luke who?
Luke at all these presents I've
brought for you!

Knock-knock.
Who's there?
Avery.
Avery who?
Avery Merry Christmas!

Knock-knock.
Who's there?
Anna.
Anna who?
Anna Happy New Year!

Knock-knock.
Who's there?
Lemmie.
Lemmie who?
Lemmie in, it's snowing!

Knock-knock.
Who's there?
Dewey.
Dewey who?
Dewey know who's coming for
Christmas dinner?

Knock-knock.
Who's there?
Howard.
Howard who?
Howard you like to come caroling
with me?

Knock-knock.
Who's there?
Interrupting Santa.
Interrupting Santa wh...
HO HO HO! MERRY CHRISTMAS!

Knock-knock.
Who's there?
Anita.
Anita who?
Anita come in, I can't wait to give you your present!

Knock-knock.
Who's there?
Elf.
Elf who?
Elf who's to small to reach the doorbell!

Knock-knock.
Who's there?
Kanye.
Kanye who?
Kanye help me put up my Christmas lights?

Knock-knock.
Who's there?
Hannah.
Hannah who?
Hannah partridge in a pear tree!

Knock-knock.
Who's there?
Walter.
Walter who?
Walter you waiting for? Open the door, and let's get Christmas started!

Knock-knock.
Who's there?
Justin.
Justin who?
Justin time for Christmas cookies!

Knock-knock.
Who's there?
Don.
Don who?
Don't open your present until Christmas,
but you can still open the door!

Knock-knock.
Who's there?
Pepper.
Pepper who?
Peppermint sticks for old St. Nick!

Knock-knock.
Who's there?
Turk.
Turk who?
Turkey with all the trimmings, let me in before it gets cold!

Knock-knock.
Who's there?
Murray.
Murray who?
Murray Christmas to all, and to all, a good night!

Section 8: Mistletoe Mysteries

Can you figure out our Christmas conundrums? Test yourself and your friends with these tantalizing teasers!

When is a boat like snow?

When it's adrift!

What famous British playwright was afraid of Christmas?

Noël Coward!

Where would you find a Christmas tree?

Between a Christmas two and a Christmas four!

How many presents can go in an empty sack?

Just one, after that, it's not empty anymore!

What falls but never gets hurt?

Snow!

I bite your toes and nip your nose and make you wear protective clothes, and yet I have no teeth – what am I?

The cold.

I look like a snowman, but I'm lighter than a feather; what am I?

A snowman's shadow!

What do donkeys call Christmas?

Mule-tide!

What is always made on Christmas Day?

A mess!

Why do Santa's reindeer fly over mountains?

Because they can't fly under them!

Which of Santa's reindeer can travel through space?

Comet!

I'm tall when I'm young and short when I'm old; what am I?

A Christmas candle.

If eleven Elves make eleven dolls in eleven minutes, how long would it take 100 elves to make 100 dolls?

Eleven minutes!

What does a Christmas tree, a Christmas turkey, and Santa's beard all have in common?

They all get trimmed at Christmas!

Section 9: 50 Festive Puns for Festive Fun

Jokes we are telling, tears of laughter are welling, the puns they are near.. It's the most pun-derful time of the year!

What do you get when you cross a cat with a Christmas tree?

A Purrrrr-tree

My brother always wears camouflage clothes at Christmas

because he doesn't want to give away his presence!

I asked my sister what she wanted for Christmas, and she said that nothing would make her happier than a new phone.

So I brought her nothing.

My Dad won the tallest Christmas tree competition this year, and I thought to myself,

"How do you top that?"

I have a knack for guessing what I got for Christmas.

It's a gift.

My little brother said he wanted a puppy for Christmas,

but Dad said he had to have turkey like everyone else!

Yule need to spruce up the tree fir Christmas.

What do you call Santa when he doesn't know where he is?

A lost Claus!

Santa is so good at delivering presents,

he sleighs!

The party in the Christmas tree was lit!

I watched a Christmas movie that was my favorite as a kid.

It was very Santa-mental for me!

My Dad brought a Santa outfit,

it suits him!

I got some fresh herbs in my stocking,

and it really felt like Christmas thyme.

My whole family has to visit my granddad over the holidays.

He always sends us a letter saying,
"Your presents is required!"

Santa's Grotto has gone off the grid,

and now they're completely elf-efficient!

Santa does listen to elves' suggestions,

but he always has the final sleigh!

Snowmen have such confidence,

because they live like snowbody's watching!

My Dad is very fussy about his Christmas candies:

he prefers them in mint condition!

Drink some warm milk and cinnamon be-fir bed on Christmas Eve,

and Yule sleep like a log!

The best Christmas present I've ever got was a broken drum,

it just can't be beat!

Beyonce has just released a new Christmas single,

All the Jingle Ladies

(If you liked it, then you should have put five gold rings on it!)

I camembert how un-brie-lievably cheesy these Christmas puns are.

But I've got to admit they are pretty Gouda!

Santa's reindeer ate all the Christmas chocolates

because they had no elf-control.

I'm going to go out on a limb and cy-press you to not to fir-get to buy the tree.

Once you get it, I'll spruce it up.

Everyone knows the main reindeer,

but no one remembers Olive, the other reindeer.

It's probably because she didn't let poor Rudolph join in any reindeer games.

My present melted?

Say it isn't snow?!

When the reindeer reins came loose one Christmas Eve,

Blitzen had to hold on for deer life!

Santa doesn't have a camera phone;

he takes North Pole-aroids!

We brought my Gran a new refrigerator for Christmas,

and we can't wait to see her face light up when she opens it!

It's getting harder and harder to find Avent Calendars.

I think their days are numbered!

What is the difference between a knight and Santa's reindeer?

One slays a dragon, and the others drag a sleigh on!

To make sure Santa can get into all the houses okay,

they have to be checked by his Elf and Safety Commission!

Santa keeps all the presents safe

in his pole vault.

What did the snowman say to Jack Frost?

Icy what you did there!

I'll be stocking up on presents
this year!

There's been a lot of accidents in Santa's workshop this year,
so Santa's had to provide elf insurance!

Snowmen can always recognize other snowmen.
It takes one to snow one!

My mum makes great hot chocolate,
but I always want myrrh!

My Gran gave me gloves for Christmas,
and I'm s-mitten!

When we went to get our Christmas tree, I saw my sister hugging a tree.

I asked her if she was okay, and she said, "I'm feeling pine!"

Santa is a real elf-made man.

My friend's family is renting their house out over Christmas;

it's for lease, Navidad!

The problem with snowmen is that they're just

a bunch of snowflakes!

Don't mess with Santa;

he's a black belt!

The North Pole is so clean because

they use a lot of Santa-tizer!

Christmas is a time when you should forget your past

and focus on your present!

My Grandad always gives me a set of spices when I see him over Christmas;

he says it's seasons greetings!

Santa has started giving the elves a book of instructions for making the toys;

it's a elf-help book!

Everyone loves Jack Frost because

he's so cool!

Everyone hated the new reindeer at first because

they heard he was a rude-elf!

Thank You Message

Thank you for reading this book; we truly hope you enjoyed it. Our aim was to help you create some lasting memories that will bring a smile to your face for years to come.

Whether it was making and eating some sweet treats, laughing at a knock-knock joke, or being surprised by an answer when playing Would You Rather, hopefully, you were able to get something positive out of the book.

Now, all that's left is to spread some festive laughter with everyone you know! After Christmas, pack the book away – along with any scorecards or written answers, so you can get it back out next year and reminisce while making new memories.

We wish you all a very Merry Christmas and a Happy New Year!

Part 2: Try Not to Laugh Christmas Challenge

Introduction Letter to Parents

Dear Guardian,

We all know the holidays are about family and fun, but we also know that connecting younger and older family members can sometimes be tricky. One thing that can unite us is humor, whether it be a belly laugh at a good joke or an eye roll about a terrible pun!

This book is geared towards bringing people together. By reading together and discussing the jokes and themes of this book, hopefully, by reading this together, you can create some lasting holiday memories and strengthen your family bond.

Our book also aims to stimulate young minds with brain teasers and jokes that will help promote lateral thinking and improve their ability to stay focused. Our questions and quizzes will help you explore the themes of Christmas and hopefully provoke discussions about what Christmas means to different people.

Humor is an important social tool, and studies have shown that kids with a well-developed sense of humor are more likely to be generally happy and optimistic, have high self-esteem, and handle differences well. Exploring humor is a great way to connect with your child, and discussions about why you did or didn't find the joke funny can allow for a greater understanding of each other. It has been proven that humor can expand cognitive capacity and enhance critical thinking skills.

Above all else, we hope the book brings you lots of laughter.

Introduction Letter to Children

Hi!

There is a lot to love about the holiday season, and it's a time for fun, friends, and family. This book is jam-packed with jokes, quizzes, and brainteasers that you can share with anyone and everyone who is special to you.

This book is made to be shared, so whether it's a crazy knock-knock joke or some Christmas trivia, our Try Not To Laugh Christmas Challenge is a great way to spend some time with your friends and family while enjoying a bit of seasonal silliness!

Challenge your family with our Christmas Quiz, share a giggle with our cheeky jokes, and test your Christmas movie knowledge with our Tinsel Town Teasers!

So grab some cookies and hang your stocking.
Put on some Christmas music that's really rocking,
Open this book to raise some good cheer,
and find jokes and laughter to last throughout the year!

Section 1: Deck the Halls with Knock-Knock Classics

Before you open your heart to Christmas, keep the door shut and unplug the doorbell so you can enjoy these nutty knock-knock jokes!

Knock-knock.
Who's there?
Mary.
Mary who?
Mary Christmas!

Knock-knock.
Who's there?
Jim.
Jim who?
Jim-gle bells, Jim-gle bells, Jim-gle all the way!

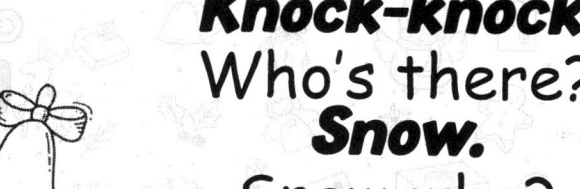

Knock-knock.
Who's there?
Snow.
Snow who?
Snow-bell, so I'm knocking!

Knock-knock.
Who's there?
Turk.
Turk who?
Turkey dinner? I'm hungry!

Knock-knock.
Who's there?
Cindy Lou.
Cindy Lou who?
Yep, that's right!

Knock-knock.
Who's there?
Elle.

Elle who?
Elle-f on the shelf, I'm back from the North Pole!

Knock-knock.
Who's there?
Honor.
Honor who?
Honor first day of Christmas, my true love sent to me!

Knock-knock.
Who's there?
Rein.
Rein who?

Rein-deer, have you seen Rudolph?

Knock-knock.
Who's there?
Chris.
Chris who?

Christmas time is here, so let me in!

Knock-Knock.
Who's there?
Olive.
Olive who?
Olive the holidays, don't you?

Knock-knock.
Who's there?
Anna.
Anna who?
Anna partridge in a pear treeeeee!

Knock-knock.
Who's there?
Oak.
Oak who?
Oak-come all ye faithful!

Knock-knock.
Who's there?

Yule.
Yule who?
Yule wanna let me in; I have gifts!

Knock-knock.
Who's there?
Ivanna.
Ivanna who?
Ivanna know what I got for
Christmas, don't you?
Knock-knock.
Who's there?
Frank.
Frank who?
Frankincense, gold, and myrrh. Are
we at the wrong stable?

Knock-knock.
Who's there?
Hoho
Hoho who?

You need to work on your Santa laugh!

Knock-knock.
Who's there?
Hosanna.
Hosanna who?
Hosanna gonna get in if you don't open the door!
Knock-knock.
Who's there?
Holly.
Holly who?
Holly-days are the best time of the year.

Knock-knock.
Who's there?
Ima.
Ima who?
Ima dreaming of a white Christmas.

Knock-knock.
Who's there?
Cal.
Cal who?

Cal me when Santa's on his way!

Knock-knock.
Who's there?
Don.
Don who?

Don't open this gift until Christmas!

Knock-knock.
Who's there?
Arthur.
Arthur who?

Arthur any cookies left?

Knock-knock.
Who's there?
Avery.
Avery who?

Avery Merry Christmas to you!

Knock-knock.
Who's there?
Tre.
Tre who?
Tre wise men; we bring gifts!

Knock-knock.
Who's there?
Olaf.
Olaf who?
Olaf at this one, please!

Knock-knock.
Who's there?
Tin soldier.
Tin soldier who?
Tin soldier who can't reach the doorbell!

Knock-knock.
Who's there?
Ivy.
Ivy who?
Ivy good mind to not give you your present if you keep me standing out here much longer!

Knock-knock.
Who's there?
Isa.

Isa who?
Isa any room at the inn?

Knock-knock.
Who's there?
Miss.
Miss who?
Mistletoe...kiss kiss!

Knock-knock.
Who's there?
Sandy.
Sandy who?
Sandy Claus; you've been good this year!

Section 2: Mistletoe Mischief - 20 Cheeky Jokes

If you have an elf on your shelf, you'll know that Christmas time can be full of mischief! Maybe your elf – or your dad – might enjoy one of these cheeky gags!

Why was the snowman looking at carrots at the grocery store?

He liked picking his own nose!

Why does the number zero hate Christmas?

Because he was on the naught-y list!

How do you know when a snowman is annoyed?

When they're frosty!

What do you call an elf wearing headphones?

Anything you want – he can't hear you!

What do you call a mean reindeer?

Rude-olph!

What do you get if you cross a sheep and a mint at Christmas?

A baaaaaaaa-humbug!

What's wrong with the Christmas alphabet?

Noel!

What happens if you get bitten by a vampire snowman?

Frostbite!

Why didn't the elf want to share?

He was elfish!

What did the elves say to Santa when he delivered all his presents in record time?

Sleigh!

Why did the elf get told off by his teacher?

He didn't do his gnomework!

Why did Santa get a parking ticket?

He left his sleigh in a snow parking zone!

What do you call an old snowman?

Water!

What do gingerbread men use when they break their legs?

They use candy canes!

What is a reindeer's favorite street food?

A donner kebab!

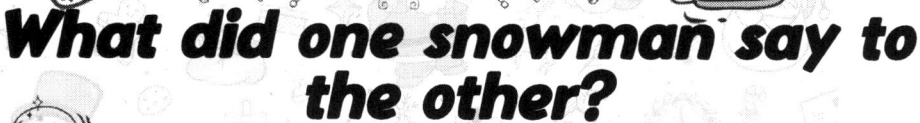

What did one snowman say to the other?

Do you smell carrots?

How does Santa know when you're awake?

He feels your presents!

What do you call Santa when he forgets his underwear?

Saint knicker-less!

What did the turkey say at Christmas?

I'm stuffed!

Why was the Christmas tree sad?

It was pining for the old days!

Section 3: 30 Cool Christmas Quiz Questions

We all love the holidays, but how well do you really know Christmas? Test yourself with this yule-tide trivia, and compete against your friends and family to determine who really is the king or queen of Christmas!

Not counting Rudolf, what were the names of Santa's reindeer?

Dasher, Dancer, Prancer, Vixen, Comet, Cupid, Donner and Blitzen.

Fun Fact: The names of Santa's reindeer were first published in 1823, and Rudolf didn't join the crew until 1939!

In the song Frosty the Snowman, what made Frosty come to life?

An old silk hat.

Fun Fact: The song Frosty the Snowman was written in 1950, and the same year, It was published as a children's book. In an animated short produced in 1969, it is revealed that the old silk hat (that must have had some magic in it) belonged to a magician called Professor Hinkle.

How many presents are given in the song The Twelve Days of Christmas?

364, if you count that a new gift is given every day along with a duplicate of the presents given the day before. If you think the singer gives one new thing every day and just recounts the gifts already given, then it would be 78! Feel free to argue that one amongst yourselves!

Fun Fact: The gifts listed are twelve drummers drumming, eleven pipers piping, ten lords a-leaping, nine ladies dancing, eight maids a-milking, seven swan- a swimming, six geese a-laying, five gold rings, four calling birds, three French hens, two turtle doves, and a partridge in a pear tree.

What date does Christmas Eve fall on?

December 24.

Fun Fact: Christmas Eve is celebrated differently all over the world. In America, kids hang up their stockings and leave cookies and milk for Santa, but in the UK, he gets a mince pie, a glass of brandy, and a carrot for the reindeer. Iceland has a Yule Book Flood, where books are exchanged to read on Christmas Eve. Many Christians across the world attend midnight Mass to celebrate the birth of Jesus, and in Denmark and Sweden, Christmas Eve is the main focus for celebration. In Australia, where Christmas falls in the middle of summer, many people head down to the beach, and in China, Christmas Eve is one of the biggest shopping days of the year.

What were the children dreaming of in the poem 'Twas the Night Before Christmas?

Dancing sugar plums.

Fun Fact: This popular poem is 200 years old!

In A Christmas Carol, what is the name of Scrooge's employee?

Bob Cratchit.

Fun Fact: In the book, Bob Cratchit is Scrooge's only employee. Scrooge's firm is called Scrooge and Marley, and they lend money to people, charging them interest on the loan.

What kind of sleigh is the singer riding in the song Jingle Bells?

A one-horse open sleigh.

Fun Fact: A one-horse open sleigh is a small vehicle with runners instead of wheels with no roof or canopy, and is small enough to be pulled by one horse. In the song, the sleigh runs into a snowbank, and the singer and his lady friend – Miss Fanny Bright – get tipped out of the sleigh!

Are Santa's reindeer boys or girls?

Despite many films suggesting that Santa's reindeer are male, bucks drop their antlers around November, so any deer that still have antlers in December as girls, meaning that Santa's reindeer must be female.

According to the song Santa Claus is Coming to Town, what does Santa know?

He knows when you're awake, and he knows if you've been bad or good.

Fun Fact: He doesn't know when you're sleeping; he sees when you're sleeping!

What color are mistletoe berries?

White.

Fun Fact: Mistletoe is associated with midwinter because it can blossom in winter, leading the Celtic Druids to link it with vitality and good luck. In Norse culture, the mistletoe was the only plant that wasn't made to swear an oath not to harm Odin's son, Baldur. Loki knew this and made an arrow from mistletoe that killed Baldur. In one tradition, Balder is resurrected, and the goddess Frigg declared that mistletoe would be a symbol of love and vowed to kiss anyone who passed under it.

How did the Three Wise Men find Jesus?

They followed a star.

Fun Fact: No one knows what the Star of Bethlehem was, but scholars have been talking about it since the 13th century. Some speculations include a supernova, a comet, a solar flare, or an alignment of planets.

What is the significance of a Yule Log?

A log known as a yule log was traditionally burned in various European countries and was a symbol of sustaining the sun god and ensuring the sun's return.

Fun Fact: The modern chocolate yule log is much tastier than the traditional one! That one tastes like sawdust!

How many times does Santa check his list, according to the song Santa Claus is Coming to Town?

Twice.

Fun Fact: Fred Astaire recorded his version of this song in 1970 when he narrated a stop-motion film with the same title.

Who's birthday is celebrated at Christmas?

Jesus'.

Fun Fact: The date of Jesus' birth isn't in the Gospels. According to those who believe that the Star of Bethlehem was an astrological conjunction of Saturn and Jupiter, Jesus was born on June 17. However, we have celebrated the birth of Jesus on December 25 since the 4th century.

Why do we hang stockings up at Christmas?

The obvious answer is to get presents, but the tradition started when the original St. Nicholas threw three bags of coins down the chimney of a poor family. The money landed in the stockings of three sisters who lived there, who had hung their stockings up to dry by the fire. In some traditions, presents are left in shoes that are beside the fire.

What gift did the Little Drummer Boy give?

He played his drum for baby Jesus.

Fun Fact: The song Little Drummer Boy is said to be based on an old Czech carol and a French carol called Patpan.

When do the Twelve Days of Christmas start?

December 25.

Fun Fact: The Twelve Days of Christmas mark the time between the birth of Jesus and the arrival of the three wise men. It begins on December 25 and lasts until January 6, which is called the Epiphany or Three King's Day.

What does Santa leave for naughty kids instead of presents?

Coal.

Fun Fact: No one really knows why Santa leaves coal for naughty kids, but many people think that when Santa comes down the chimney, he grabs a lump of coal out of the fireplace just because it is close by. As we don't tend to use coal fires now, what do you think Santa might put in the stocking of someone who has been naughty?

What kind of houses are only made at Christmas?

Gingerbread houses.

Fun Fact: Gingerbread houses were first made in Germany in the 16th century and became popular after the Brothers Grimm wrote Hansel and Gretel, although no one knows if the story or the treat came first.

What usually goes on the top of a Christmas Tree?

A star, an angel, or a fairy.

Fun Fact: No one knows where tree-toppers originated, but they were first recorded in Germany in the Seventeenth century when baby Jesus tree-toppers were popular.

How many windows are in an advent calendar?

Twenty-four. Unless you get a special one that gives you an extra window for Christmas Day!

Fun Fact: Advent actually begins on the fourth Sunday before Christmas and is celebrated on each Sunday leading up to Christmas, which is why some Advent wreaths have four candles. Because there is no fixed start date, it means that Advent is a different length each year. However, as Advent Calendars are either reused or mass-produced, it is easier to count from December 1.

What gifts did the Three Wise Men give to baby Jesus?

Gold, Frankincense, and Myrrh.

Fun Fact: Gold represented Jesus' being the king of the Jews, frankincense signified his divinity, and myrrh was a reminder of his mortality and that he would die for the sins of humanity.

Before electric lights, what did people put on their Christmas tree?

Candles.

Fun Fact: Trees and light have been linked since the Pagan times. When people started to bring Christmas trees into their homes, they would secure candles to the branches with wire, string, needles, or counterweight candle holders. In 1878, the clip-on candle holder was invented and was used right up until the mid-20th century. However, because of the obvious fire risk, the candles were only lit for a maximum of 30 minutes and had to be watched carefully with buckets of water on standby!

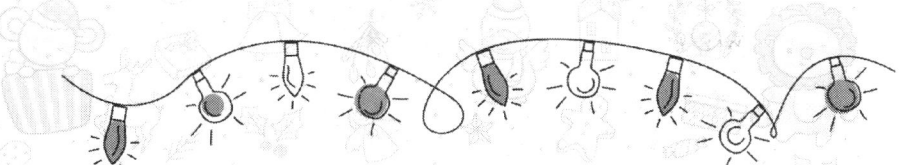

What was Frosty the Snowman's nose made out of?

A button.

Fun Fact: Snowmen's eyes are usually made of coal or stones, but their nose isn't always a carrot. Frosty's nose was a button, and the nose of the snowman in the 1982 animated film The Snowman was a tangerine!

What kind of Christmas did Elvis have?

A Blue Christmas.

Where was Jesus born?

In Bethlehem.

Fun Fact: The Church of the Nativity was built on top of a cave in Bethlehem where people believe Jesus was born and is listed by UNESCO as having outstanding universal value.

How many ghosts visited Scrooge on Christmas Eve?

Four. The ghosts of Christmas past, present, future, and – of course – Scrooge's old partner Jacob Marley.

What ornament is hidden on a Christmas tree that people have to find?

A pickle.

Fun Fact: Many families across America hang an ornament in the shape of a pickle from their tree. The first to find the pickle on Christmas morning either gets to open a present first or gets an extra present. When the tradition started, many believed that it originated in Germany; however, the Germans had never heard of it!

What ballet has the Sugar Plum Fairy as a character?

The Nutcracker.

Fun Fact: A sugar plum was originally made by coating a fruit or a nut in layers of sugar, but soon, it became a name to describe any small, round candy. Eventually, sugar plums became a symbol of everything sweet and yummy, which is why Tchaikovsky made the Sugar Plum Fairy the ruler of the Land of Sweets.

What other names does Santa Claus go by?

St. Nicholas, Kris Kringle, Father Christmas.

Fun Fact: St. Nicholas was the original bearer of gifts and was called Sinterklaas by the Dutch (from which we get Santa Claus). Kris Kringle is an anglicized version of *Christkindl*, meaning Christ

Child and the name Father Christmas comes from the medieval idea of Christmas personified.

Section 4: Snowman Stand Up: 20 Classic Christmas Funnies

Why was the snowman great at stand-up? Because he couldn't sit down!

You definitely won't get a frosty reception with these glorious gags. In fact, you'll be such a star you won't be able to stop wise men from following you!

Joseph and Mary knew Jesus's weight straight **away because they had a** weigh in the manger!

At Frosty the Snowman's birthday, everyone always sings,

"Freeze a jolly good fellow, and snow say all of us!"

Then he gets the bumpety bump bump bumpety bump bumps!

After Mary thanked the three wise men for the gold and frankincense, they said,

"Wait…there's myrrh!"

I really don't like it when Santa visits…

I think I've got

claus-trophobia!

What kind of key let Mary and Joseph into the stable?

A donkey!

Whenever Santa's helpers get ill,

he nurses them back to elf!

What do you call the ghost of a reindeer?

A Cari-boo!

What happens when you don't let a snowman get his way?

He has a meltdown!

What reindeer games do the other reindeer play?

Truth or deer!

Santa's great at going down chimneys;

it really soots him!

COVID didn't affect the North Pole because they

used plenty of Santa-tizer!

Santa's sleigh didn't cost any money because

it was on the house!

Why are Christmas toys so Zen?

Because they live in the present!

What do you call candies you put on the Christmas tree?

Orna-mints!

Did you hear about the guy who stole the advent calendar?

He got 25 days!

Where do Christmas elves keep their money?

In a snow bank!

What do elves use to make s'mores?

Christmas crackers!

What falls but doesn't get hurt?

Snow!

The weather on Christmas Eve is so bad because

there's a 100% chance of rain, deer!

Who delivers presents to baby sharks?

Santa Jaws!

Section 5: Festive Would You Rather

Christmas is usually a time for getting what you want, but what if you had to choose? Compare your answers with your friends and family, or turn this section into a game by trying to guess what others would choose!

How well do you know your friends? Write down what you think they will say on a card and put it face down on the table. Once your friend gives their answer, turn your card over and see if they match

Would you rather only eat cabbage or reindeer corn for the entire holiday season?

Would you rather have elf ears or Santa's beard?

Would you rather eat turkey that tastes like candy canes or candy canes that tastes like turkey?

Would you rather have a stocking full of jelly or a Christmas cracker full of custard?

Would you rather have a stocking full of jelly or a Christmas cracker full of custard?

Would you rather wear an ugly sweater or a hat made of tinsel all Christmas?

Would you rather eat dry turkey or raw parsnips?

Would you rather be friends with Frosty the Snowman or Buddy the Elf?

Would you rather have candy canes for fingers or baubles for ears?

Would you rather – if you only had ONE choice –watch The Grinch or The Christmas Chronicles?

Would you rather have ten lords a-leaping or nine ladies dancing over for Christmas dinner?

Would you rather open all your presents on Christmas Eve or wait until Christmas Day?

Would you rather have a red nose like Rudolph or be covered in green hair like the Grinch?

Would you rather be a Christmas toy tester or a Christmas candy taster?

Would you rather have Christmas trees for legs or Christmas crackers for arms?

Would you rather help Santa make the toys or deliver the presents?

Would you rather eat a gingerbread house or live in one?

Would you rather have no Christmas lights or no Christmas tree?

Would you rather look after Santa's reindeer or his elves?

Would you rather travel to the North Pole on the Polar Express or on a flying reindeer?

Would you rather have a nose made out of a carrot or eyes made of coal?

Would you rather have three French hens or a partridge in a pear tree?
Would you rather eat figgy pudding or a mince pie?

Would you rather fight one snowman-sized elf or ten elf-sized snowman?

Would you rather end every sentence singing, "And all I want for Christmas is you!" Or start every sentence by singing, "Last Christmas, I gave you my heart."

Would you rather your family have to wear matching Christmas sweaters or matching Christmas pajamas?

Would you rather go dashing through the snow in a one-horse sleigh or be roasting chestnuts on an open fire?

Would you rather have to dodge 100 small snowballs or one giant snowball?

Would you rather have no Christmas dinner or no dessert?

Would you rather have turkey with syrup for breakfast or pancakes and gravy for dinner?

Would you rather have a nose like a cherry or a little round

belly that shakes when you laugh like a bowlful of jelly?

Would you rather be able to turn into a Christmas fairy or a magic snowman?

Would you rather have to clean Santa's workshop or the reindeer's barn?

Would you rather play in snow made of ice cream or snow made of marshmallows?

Would you rather listen to "We Wish You a Merry Christmas" on repeat for a week or sing it once in front of your whole school?

Would you rather only have hot chocolate or hot cider to drink for the whole month of December?

Section 6: Tinsel Town Teasers: 20 Movie-Themed Questions

Perhaps one of the best things about Christmas is getting into some elastic-waisted trousers and settling down to watch a Christmas movie while snacking on Christmas treats. We all love a good Christmas movie, and if we're honest, most of us love the bad ones, too! Test your family's festive movie knowledge with these questions, and get some inspiration for what movie Gran will fall asleep to next!

According to Buddy the Elf, what are the four major food groups?

Candy, Candy Corn, Candy Cane, and Syrup.

Fun Fact: In the film, Buddy eats a breakfast of spaghetti topped with candies, marshmallows, maple syrup, and chocolate sauce. The really strange thing is that people have created multiple recipes for this crazy meal! One restaurant in Chicago even added it to their menu, calling it a Spaghetti Sundae!

What did the burglars in Home Alone call themselves?

The Wet Bandits in the first Home Alone and the Sticky Bandits in the second film

Fun Fact: In the film, Marv comes up with the name and leaves taps running in the houses they break into as a "calling card." Because of this, the police can identify every house that they robbed. In the second Home Alone, he wraps double-sided sticky tape around his hands to help him steal from a donation bucket.

What is the name of the magical train that goes to the North Pole?

The Polar Express.

What song does Santa sing while in jail in the film The Christmas Chronicles?

Santa Claus is Back in Town.

Fun Fact: The song was first recorded by Elvis in 1957.

What type of kids Christmas movies were popular in the 1960s, 70s and 80s?

Claymation

Fun Fact: Tim Burton reprised the classic stop motion Claymation technique in his spooky Christmas/Halloween crossover classic The Nightmare Before Christmas.

According to Buddy the Elf, what is the best way to spread Christmas cheer?

Singing loud for all to hear.

What do the candy canes allow people to do in Santa Claus the Movie?

They allow people to fly.

Fun Fact: All the toys made and brought for this 1985 movie were donated to children's charities after the shooting was complete.

What is the main character's name in The Santa Clause?

Scott Calvin.

What toy is everyone after in Jingle All the Way?

A Turbo-Man action figure.

What is the highest-grossing Christmas movie of all time?

Home Alone.

Fun Fact: Home Alone grossed $476.7 million worldwide.

Who is the villain in The Santa Clause 3?

Jack Frost.

In A Muppets Christmas Carol, who is Gonzo playing?

Charles Dickens.

Fun Fact: Charles Dickens wrote A Christmas Carol in just six weeks because he needed to make some money! Many of our ideas about what makes an "ideal Christmas" come from Dickens. The image of a white snowy Christmas is due to eight unusually harsh winters that Dickens had experienced as a child, and the holiday's focus on charity and giving is largely down to the Dickensian Christmas.

How many sizes too small was the Grinch's heart?

Two.

In the short film Robin Robin, what animals raised the baby Robin?

Mice.

Fun Fact: Robins work for Santa, which is why they have red chests. In England, robins don't migrate so that they can keep an eye on the boys and girls all year. They move around a bit more in America but don't always fly south in the winter like other birds. If you see a robin, make sure you're being nice because they are sure to let Father Christmas know what you're up to!

What is the main character's name in the film A Christmas Story?

Ralphie Parker.

In what city did Kevin McCallister get lost in Home Alone 2?

New York.

Fun Fact: This film features the 45th American president, Donald Trump.

What is Olaf searching for in Olaf's Frozen Adventure?

Christmas traditions.

In the film Klaus, what is Jesper's job?

Postman.

What is the present that gets missed in Arthur Christmas?

A bicycle.

Bonus Point: The present was for Gwen, who lives in Trelew, Cornwall.

How many Home Alone movies have been made?

As of 2023, there have been six Home Alone movies,

however there is a rumor that the original star – Macaulay Culkin – will return for a sequel.

Section 7: Holiday Feast Funnies: 20 Fantastic Food Jokes

Aside from the presents, spending time with family, and the awesome decorations, one thing that defines Christmas is eating too much, complaining about being full, and then tucking into the box of Christmas chocolates! So enjoy this feast of hilarity while munching your way through the Christmas cookies!

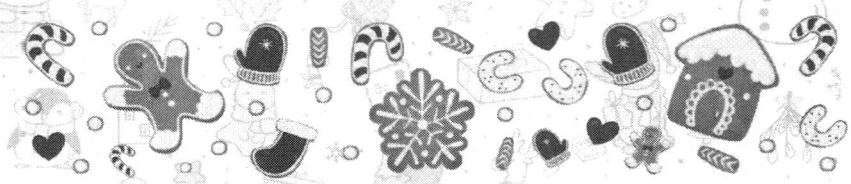

Did you hear about the guy who fell into a Christmas pudding?

He was dragged in by a strong currant!

What do you call it when a family passes down a turkey recipe?

Copy and baste!

Why did the mad scientist cross a turkey with a centipede?

So everyone could have a leg!

If fruit comes from palm trees, where does turkey come from?

Poul-tree!

I love the meat and vegetables at Christmas dinner, and the rest is just gravy!

I think my brother hates turkey at Christmastime; he always tells me it's fowl!

How does good King Wenceslas like his pizza?

Deep pan, crisp, and even!

What sneaks into the kitchen at Christmas?

Mince spies!

My Mom says the key to a really good Christmas dinner is the tur-key!

What is the math teacher's favorite holiday food?

Apple Pi!

When are toes allowed on the Christmas table?

When they're pota-toes!

How does Darth Vader like his turkey?

On the dark side.

How do Santa's elves make Christmas cakes?

They use elf-raising flour!

Why couldn't the teddy bear finish his Christmas dinner?

Because he was full of stuffing!

How does Jack Frost like his cakes?

With plenty of frosting!

What did one cranberry say to the other cranberry at Christmas?

'Tis the season to be jelly!

What's red and white and blue at Christmas?

A sad candy cane!

My family was supposed to have a traditional German dessert for Christmas this year, but it was stollen!

What's the best thing to put into a Christmas cake?

Your teeth!

When is a candy cane worth the most?

When it's in mint condition!

Section 8: 30 Festive Quotes for All!

If Christmas were a person, their ears would be burning! Here is proof that Christmas may be the most talked about holiday, and some tips on how you can spread Christmas cheer far and wide for all to hear!

It's Christmas Eve. A time of mystery, expectations, who knows what might happen?

The Nutcracker and the Four Realms

Christmas is the season for kindling the fire of hospitality.

Washington Irving

Christmas is here again. Let us raise a loving cup, peace on

earth, goodwill to men, and make them do the washing up!

Wendy Cope

I think this Christmas thing is not as tricky as it seems, and why should they have all the fun?

It should belong to everyone!

The Nightmare Before Christmas

Wrap yourself up in each other's presence and don't just submerge yourself in the presents.

Anonymous

Just remember the true spirit of Christmas lies in your heart.

The Polar Express

Nothing's as mean as giving a little child something useful for Christmas!

Ken Hubbard

The worst gift is fruitcake. There is only one fruitcake in the entire world, and people keep sending it to each other!

Johnny Carson

I once brought my kids a set of batteries for Christmas with a note on it saying, "Toys not included!"

Bernard Manning

Christmas isn't a season; it's a feeling.

Edna Ferber

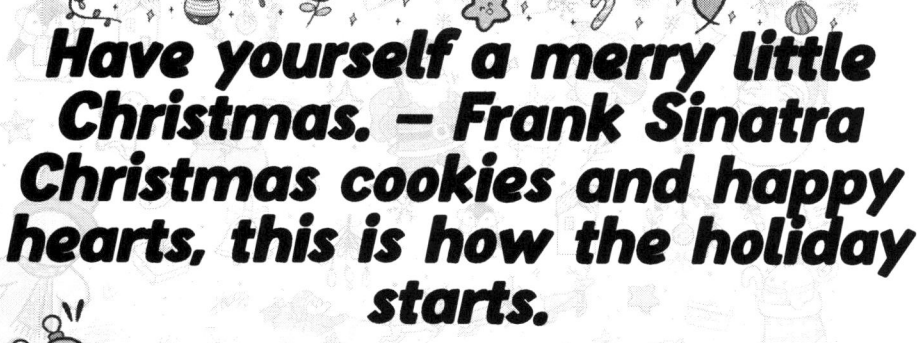

Have yourself a merry little Christmas. – Frank Sinatra Christmas cookies and happy hearts, this is how the holiday starts.

Anonymous

The way you spend Christmas is far more important than how much.

Henry David Thoreau

Christmas is crazy. It's the only time of year when you're excited for someone to break into your house, and then you eat the candy they put in your socks.

Anonymous

You can mess with a lot of things. But you can't mess with kids on Christmas!

Home Alone 2: Lost in New York

It's beginning to look a lot like Christmas, toys in every store, but the prettiest sight to see is the holly that will be on your own front door.

Andy Williams.

The three phrases that sum up Christmas are: Peace on Earth, Goodwill to Men, and Batteries not Included!

Anonymous

I will honor Christmas in my heart and try to keep it all the year.

A Christmas Carol

Gifts of time and love are surely the basic ingredients of a truly merry Christmas.

Peg Bracken

One of the most glorious messes in the world is the mess created in the living room on Christmas Day. Don't clean it up too quickly.

Andy Rooney

When we recall Christmas past, we usually find that the simplest things – not the great occasions – give off the greatest glow of happiness.

Bob Hope

He who has not Christmas in his heart will never find it under a tree.

Roy L. Smith

Oh come all ye faithful, joyful, and triumphant...

John Francis Wade

Kissin' by the mistletoe, love came to stay, and now it's Christmas every day.

Aretha Franklin

Unless we make Christmas an occasion to share our blessings, all the snow in Alaska won't make it "white."

Bing Crosby

Now the God of Hope fill you with all the joy and peace in believing that ye may abound in hope, through the power of the Holy Ghost.

Romans 15:13, Bible, King James Version.

Love the giver more than the gift.

Brigham Young

It's the most wonderful time of the year.

Edward Pola and George Wyle

And so I'm offering this simple phrase to kids from one to ninety-two. Although it's been said many times, many ways, Merry Christmas to you.

Nat King Cole

Happy Christmas to all, and to all, a good night!

The Night Before Christmas

Section 9: Wrapped in Whimsy: 20 Festive Puns

Yule love this selection of Christmas puns! Most of them are real crackers, although you may find a few that are like Rudolf when he hurt his leg playing reindeer games: lame!

I went to the choose-and-cut farm yesterday, but it was a real tree-for-all, and I just couldn't cut it!

When the Christmas lights are on, you know the party is going to be LIT!

Christmas is a time to forget your past and concentrate on your present!

You wood not believe this, but my tree is artificial!

My favorite Ghost of Christmas is the Ghost of Christmas Presents.

I always go for a fir tree at Christmas, but this year, I think I'm going to branch out.

Santa put me on the naughty list. To be fair, he did have just Claus.

I love it when we get our Christmas tree. It really spruces the place up, but what I love the most is choosing the tree; I'll never fir get it. Even thinking about it has me feeling pine!

What does Mrs. Claus say to Santa before he goes out to deliver presents? I love you from your sled to your mistletoes!

What Snowmen do in their spare time is snowbody's business.

Santa's helpers always have their phones with them because they love taking elfies and checking snow-cial media.

Most of Santa's reindeer are cool, but that one with the red nose is super rude-olf.

I've had my Christmas stocking since I was a kid; it's really santa-mental to me.

If you're naughty, you get coal – that's Claus and Effect!

At Christmas, it's a tradition in my house to do laundry after dark because, in that Christmas carol, the shepherds washed their socks by night.

If everyone thinks the Christmas star is so great, why has it only got three followers?

It might be time to get a new Christmas stocking. The old one is hanging on by a thread!

How did Mrs. Claus know that the reindeer were close? She herd them!

Christmas is a time when you really have to treat yo' elf!

When I'm feeling a bit anxious, I go and visit Jack Frost. He's just so chill!

My Christmas celebrations started small, but they just snowballed!

Section 10: 30 Christmas Tongue Twisters

Ever the slickest elf will struggle to say these festive tongue twisters! Challenge your friends and family to find out who can say it the fastest!

Six sick snowmen sneezing sniffily!

Vixen and Blitzen love kittens in mittens!

Seven stripy stockings stuffed with sweets!

Santa sleds in the snow; if there's no snow, how does the sled go?

Crunchy crisp Christmas cookies cooling in the kitchen.

How many deer would a reindeer ride if a reindeer could ride deer?

Seven skiing snowmen sing several silly songs!

It rains in the lane dear, on the Christmas reindeer, isn't it a shame dear to see reindeer in the rain dear!

Santa's suit has Chimney soot all along the sleeves; the soot

sat on the suit and made
Santa sneeze.

Frosty freezes frequently,
feeling fairly fine!

Presents presented perfectly,
particularly please people!

Holly hangs here happily.

Tired tree trimmers try to trim
trees, but tree trimming is
tough to tired tree trimmers!

Rudolf, the Red-Nosed
Reindeer, races, running rings
around the rest of the
reindeer.

Ten tiny toy tin trains toot on the track.

Santa's sled slides on the slick snow.

Kris Kringle cooks candy canes and Christmas cookies!

They stared at a star from afar, but how far was the star that they stared at?

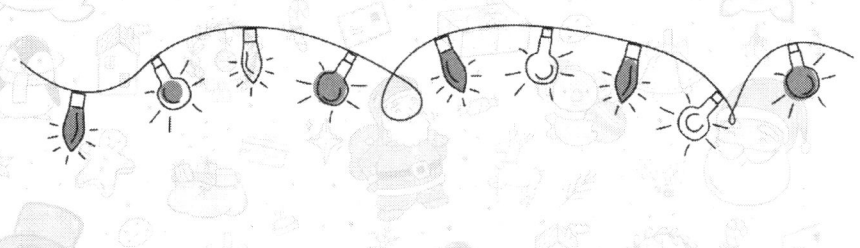

Who can crack a Christmas cracker quicker? The quickest Christmas cracker cracker can crack a Christmas cracker quicker!

A roll of rubbish wrapping rips while rolling, and a rubbish-ripping wrapping roll ruins rapid wrapping!

Twelve tall, twinkling trees totally trimmed with tinsel.

Soft and silent snowflakes settle in the starlight.

Eleven elite-elected elves elaborate elusively.
Santa slips his sack silently from his sleigh and sneaks, secretly slipping sweets into stockings!

Tasty turkey, crispy cookie, tasty turkey, crispy cookie!

Elves eat anything except easter eggs!

Rudolf wraps wreaths wrong!

Santa slips on his slippers and sips spiced cider.
Fabulously festive fairies frolic freely!

Calm, cozy Christmas candles can cause contentment.

Section 11: Silly Song Lyrics

Most of us know the popular Christmas songs back-to-front and inside-out, so we've switched up the lyrics to these well-known festive tunes to make them super silly. Can you think of your own funny lyrics? To make this into a game, pick a song that everyone has to alter. The person who gets the most laughs wins!

Jingle Bells, Batman Smells,
An egg did Robin lay,
The Batmobile lost a wheel,
And the Joker got away!

Frosty the Snowman, stood outside my home,

I sprayed him with some cherry fizz, and now he's a snow cone!

Frosting and marzipan make a very tasty cake,

I make sure mine's from the grocery store because I cannot bake!

Rudolf, the Red Nose Reindeer, likes to wear designer clothes,

He wants to be a model, and he loves to strike a pose!

Then, one smoggy Christmas Eve, Santa came to say,

He said Rudolph, with your clothes, so right,

Won't you style my elves tonight?

Then, how the elves all loved it; in their new designer threads,

They shut down toy production, and now they're making clothes instead!

O Christmas pee O Christmas pee, I really need a Christmas pee!

I promise I won't be long,

Just one pee, and then I'm done,

But now, maybe I'll grab a cookie; I hope Santa doesn't see!

While Shepherds wash their socks by night,

All seated round the tub,

The Angel of the Lord came down,

And gave their socks a scrub!

When they got to Bethlehem,

Their socks all nice and neat,

Mary said you've got nice socks,

But next time, wash your feet!

On the twelfth day of Christmas, my enemy gave to me,

Twelve colds a' coming,

Eleven Grinchs griping,

Ten alarms a'beeping,

Nine carollers singing,

Eights cold fries from Burger King,

Seven Christmas lights dimming,

Six kids complaining,

FIVE unwise kings!

Four pooping birds,

Three mangey hens,

Two thread-bare gloves,

And a pantry with empty shelves!

My childhood was frightful,

Although my sister's just delightful

And now everywhere is covered in snow,

Let it go! Let it go! Let it go!

My powers we tried stopping,

My dad, he was a top king,

His death was a horrible blow,

Let it Go! Let it Go! Let it Go!

My sister's first kiss was tonight

It really kicked up a storm

But she can't marry him, right?

I said no, and now I'm truly torn

So, I built an ice tower while crying

And there's definitely no denying

That everywhere is covered in snow

Let it go! Let it go! Let it go!

We wish you a merry citrus,

We wish you a merry citrus,

We wish you a merry citrus,

And grapefruit, orange!

Good nectarines we bring,

And some lemon,

We wish you a merry citrus,

And grapefruit orange!

We'll bring you some limes and clementines,

We'll bring you some limes and clementines,

Oh, we'll bring you some limes and clementines,

And we won't get scurvy!

But we won't go until we've got plums,

No, We won't go until we've got plums,

No, we won't go until we've got plums,

We want plum cobbler!

We hope you liked our book so jolly, ha ha ha ha ha ha ha ha ha!

If you didn't, then we are sorry! Ha ha ha ha ha ha ha ha ha!

Won't you sing this funny carol, ha ha ha ha ha ha ha ha ha!

Crazier than monkeys in a barrel, ha ha ha ha ha ha ha ha ha!

Thank You Message

Thank you for reading and sharing this book.

We hope that you've been able to enjoy some of the seasonal merriment and that you've spread the joy of the season far and wide.

It's important to remember that this time of year can be tough for some people, but sharing a smile and a silly joke can often help to raise people's spirits and create connections that inspire joy and happiness.

The intention of this book is to help you make some Christmas memories that will always make you smile.

Perhaps Dad picked a hilariously unexpected answer in Would You Rather, or Mum was surprisingly good at Christmas Trivia. Maybe you made a friend snort with laughter at a funny joke, or your older sister couldn't help but raise a smile between eye-rolls! Whatever you take from this book, our hope is that it made you laugh and contributed to the joy of your Christmas holidays.

To quote the Muppets:
It is the season of the spirit; the message, if we hear it, is make it last all year!

Printed in Great Britain
by Amazon

54157590R00117